DEAD FALL

Brad D. Sibbersen

FIRST

In the days when the world was new, the sun, called Haioo, did not move across the sky, but shone steadily, motionless, continually blessing the First People of the world and all the world's creatures with His light and warmth. But many among the First People were displeased with Haioo, for his ever-present heat burnt the skin red, until it remained this color forever, and His brightness worried the eyes when it was time for rest, so that they could not sleep, and his ever-present light revealed the hunter to his prey, allowing the deer and the rabbit to escape even the swiftest of arrows. So the First People called upon their finest warrior, a young man of the Luccee tribe, who fashioned a terrible spear out of a single, great bone and hurled this into the heart of Haioo, mortally wounding Him. Haioo's fiery blood rained from the sky for days and days, staining the land as far as the eye could see. Then Haioo Himself slid from the sky, plunging the world into eternal darkness, bringing unbearable cold and starvation and death. The First People wept and lamented for many weeks, until the Creator of All was moved to resurrect Haioo and return Him to His place in the sky, on the condition that He only light the world for a portion of each day, so that the People would no longer take Him for granted. And from that moment on, they did not. Nevertheless, once a year Haioo perishes again, painting the leaves red-orange with his blood as he sinks lower and lower in the sky, dying only to be reborn again, an eternal reminder of the hubris of the First People. For this reason the third season is forever a season that belongs to the dying and the dead, and, if they so desire, they may return during this time to do their mischief upon the People.

THEN

It had been hard, sweaty work, the late August sun beating down like a taskmaster with a chip on his shoulder, baking them in their own skin from just after sunup until it dipped behind the line of pine trees to the west, finally affording some relief as it draped them in shadows. Samuel had worked harder than most, taking no breaks, directing other work from a distance even as he completed tasks of his own, foregoing lunch and subsisting entirely on warm water carried up from the stream.

He had never been happier.

The bell, that had been the hardest part. Liberated from its original home at the abandoned train depot five miles away, it had taken them all day to pull it down and manhandle it around town (trundling it directly through town was, of course, out of the question), through the woods, down the steep hill (it almost got away from them here – what a sight that would have been!) and up the narrow staircase into the steeple. But it had been worth it. The white man who owned the property the depot now sat on had told them that they could have the bell, free of charge, if they collected it immediately and did the work themselves. So they did.

And now their church had its own bell.

Samuel silently raised a single beefy arm and all work ceased, people gratefully plopping down where they stood, finally pausing to wipe the day's sweat from their brows. They were a fine congregation. Devout. Hard working. And now, with God's grace, it was finally happening. A place of their own. To worship. To gather. To...

"Reverend Samuel," one of the women said, pointing.

There were three whites, on horseback, watching them from the top of the hill.

No, four.

Five.

More kept coming.

"Samuel!" their leader shouted down. Samuel frowned. He knew the man well. Unfortunately. *"We done tole you we don't want no nigra church in this town. Which o' them plain English words don't you understand?"*

Samuel didn't respond. No answer would satisfy these men. But he stood his ground. At nearly seven feet, he was intimidating. Enough to give even this many whites – a score of them now – pause.

His congregation was more easily cowed. They shrank back, prepared to flee.

"Buncha God-fearing niggers," the man went

on. *"When you should be fearin' us."*

Some of them had torches, Samuel realized. They meant to burn his church. His large, calloused hands curled into fists.

"I'd git if I were you, Samuel," a second white said, almost apologetically. "Let us do what we come to do."

"No," he said quietly, to himself.

The white men waited a beat and then their leader shrugged.

"Okay, then. **Yah!**" He spurred his horse down the hill and the others followed. But they didn't whoop or holler, which was somehow more intimidating than if they had. The congregation scattered, bolting in all directions across the clearing and melting into the surrounding wood like shadows.

Samuel did not flee. He waited, defiantly, as they rode straight towards him. His only concession was a prayer, mouthed silently. He closed his eyes and folded his hands, but he didn't kneel, which he'd always felt was proper – well-nigh mandatory – when addressing the Lord. He didn't want the whites to misinterpret this and think, even for a moment, that he was pleading with *them.*

He was sure that God would understand.

LATER

–I–

"See, there's *two* universes," Deacon said, endeavoring to explain the episode of *Super Friends* he was watching. "And *this* Superman comes from a universe where everyone is *evil*." He assumed this was a concept his grandmother would have some difficulty with, but she waved a dismissive hand like he was preaching to the converted.

"It's the same old story," she said. "There's always a rotten version of the hero who shows up to test his mettle. And he always comes from someplace crazy!"

Now Deacon was the one who was confused.

"*Metal* because Superman's the Man of Steel?" he asked.

"Not *metal*, dear. *Mettle*. It means..."

"Mom, have you seen my small suitcase?"

"It's in the car already," the old woman sighed.

"Deak, we're leaving as soon as your show is over, okay?"

"'Kay."

Elise tousled her grandson's hair and joined her daughter in the kitchen, where the younger woman was loading sandwiches and sodas into a cooler.

"It's not right," she said.

"Mom, enough."

"He's twelve years old. A boy his age should be in school."

"Home schooling is better than public school, believe me. He's going to have a private tutor for Christ's sake."

"'Private tutor'," scoffed Elise. "You mean that beatnik?"

"He's not a beatnik," Erin said, rolling her eyes.

"Well, a hippie then. It's 1979, Erin. That whole hippie thing, it's not even a thing anymore. All the TV programs, the police shows, the rotten ones are always hippies. Hippies and bikers. That's when you know a movement has run its course, when it starts turning up on all the TV shows."

"Mother, *please*."

"I don't like it," Elise said.

"What do you want me to do? Go back to Craig?" She lowered her voice. "Wait for him to start knocking Deak around the way he knocked me around?"

"You could stay here..."

"There's no *room* here, Mom. And you can't afford us."

"You could get a job! I could watch Deacon during the day while you were at your job...!" She was fretting now, rehashing old arguments, grasping at straws. The conversation was over.

"Mom." Erin put her hands on her mother's shoulders. "This is going to be good for us. For Deak. Spiritual."

"'Spiritual'," Elise scoffed again.

Erin drew her in and forced a hug out of her.

–II–

"...if rock's your game it's KISS!"

Deacon had been singing the jingle repeatedly since they'd left. Some doll based on a rock star, advertised incessantly during his cartoons. Exactly the sort of pointless consumerism she wanted to limit his exposure to. Well, there'd be no TV at Asylum, she assumed. Maybe no electricity. Back to nature. Minimalism. Wisdom. Spirituality.

Everything life in the poisoned suburbs had siphoned out of them.

"Maybe we could listen to some different music now?" Erin suggested.

"The 8-track's broken," Deacon said.

"The radio works. Let's listen to the radio."

"Okay."

She found a country music station.

"Mom, is it nice in Ohio?"

She smiled.

"It is. It's cool and crisp, and the leaves are beautiful this time of year, and where we'll be there won't be any noise or pollution. There'll be all sorts of animals – you like animals – and places to explore and cookouts..."

"Why is it called Asylum? That's a place for crazy people."

"No, an asylum is someplace you go to feel safe. So when... *crazy*... people are put in a hospital where they're safe, they call it an asylum. See?"

"I guess."

They rode in silence for a while.

"Are we going to Asylum to be safe from Dad?"

The question was like an acid-punch to the guts. God, how much did he know? How much had he seen, or overheard?

No point in lying to him now.

"Yeah," she said, taking his hand and squeezing it. "Yeah."

–III–

The trip took twenty-seven hours, but there was no money for a hotel so Erin drove straight through, hitting the occasional rest stop so they could munch on the sandwiches she'd packed or grab a few minutes of restless sleep. She still had twenty dollars left when they crossed the Ohio state line, so she stopped in some inconsequential speck of a town and bought Deacon a few comic books – *Superman, Fantastic Four, The Micronauts.* Something to help pass the time as he adjusted to their new life. They wouldn't need money where they were going, so she spent the remainder on sodas. She had a mild caffeine addiction she wanted to ease herself off of.

The highway eventually gave way to a local

road, and this to an unpaved dirt road that led them deep into a wood exploding with color. "Wow!" said Deacon, more than once, and she smiled. He'd never experienced this kind of autumnal splendor in Phoenix. She expected the barely-a-road they were now following to slowly peter out, and which point they'd probably have to walk, but then, unexpectedly, they found themselves on pavement again. Poorly-maintained pavement, but pavement, nonetheless. Erin was baffled. She double-checked her directions. Her understanding was that...

"Mom. Look."

She looked up at the sound of Deacon's voice and slowed the car to a stop.

It wasn't Asylum. It was *an* asylum.

Huge, imposing even in its decrepitude, the second and third stories leaned heavily to the left, as if ready to slide to the ground where they could finally get some rest. The road they were following, rutted, cracked, grass poking through, snaked right through the front gates and ended at a triple set of weather-beaten, tiered stairs leading to the front door. One of the heavy wrought iron gates was fully open, flush against the low concrete wall that surrounded the place, the other hung at an angle, barely supported by a single, unbroken hinge.

Erin turned the engine off and got out. There was a lighter, less-weathered rectangle on the wall where a sign had obviously once been mounted, but it the sign was gone, the bolts securing it torn right out of the concrete.

"Is this it?" Deacon asked from the car.

"No, honey, I don't think this is it. I think we're lost."

"Hello!" someone called out. A girl barely out of her teens, with dyed, platinum-blonde hair that had grown out to reveal dark brown roots, was walking down the drive. She had one of those scrunchy, pinched faces that rarely age well, and her shorts were far too short for late October, despite the warm midday sun.

"I think we're lost," Erin told the girl.

"No," the girl said. "You've just been found."

$$-IV-$$

Asylum, it turned out, was, well, behind the asylum.

"You're lucky I was in the Building," Keloli explained as they followed a winding trail through the woods. "That's what we call it," she explained. "'The Building'. Adam doesn't like words like 'hospital' or 'institution'. Thinks they're toxic."

Erin nodded. Deacon trudged along behind, ignoring them, immersed in one of his new comic books.

"Keloli," she said. "That's an unusual name."

"It's Kellie, actually. Kellie Norton. Keloli is my rebirth name. You'll get one too, eventually."

Erin nodded again.

"No one lives in the Building," Keloli went on.

"We each have our own cabin. Well, for now. Once we get more converts we'll have to start doubling up."

"Or we could build more cabins," Erin suggested. Keloli laughed.

"We didn't build *these*," she explained. "They used to be part of a summer camp or something. Went bankrupt in the 1960s."

"But the Collective owns the land right? I mean, we're not... squatting?"

"We own all of this!" Keloli said, twirling and sweeping her arms around for emphasis. "The Building included. Well, Adam owns it, technically. His parents left it to him. I guess they planned on developing the land and just never got around to it. But everything here is communal, so as long as you're one of us, you own it too."

"Do I own it too?" asked Deacon, finally looking up from his comic.

"You do!" Keloli beamed. "Neat, huh?"

The eight prefab cabins sat in a clearing overlooked by a steepish hill and surrounded by trees awash in oranges, reds, and yellows. Scattered in a carefully planned haphazard manner, they were all roughly equidistant from a central gathering place, where the remnants of a large fire smoldered.

"What's that noise?" asked Deacon.

"That gurgling? There's a river, just on the other side of those trees." Keloli pointed it out.

"More of a glorified stream, really, but the water's fresh, and clean. A gift from nature."

"Where is everyone?" Erin asked.

"Meditating. It's quiet time. I'd be in my cabin too, but I had to..." She trailed off, but Erin didn't notice.

"Which one's ours?" asked Deacon.

"They're *all* yours," Keloli smiled. "But you'll be *staying* in Number Six. Is that okay with you?" She leaned forward, hands on her knees, so that she was eye-to-eye with the boy. He stared for several seconds before answering.

"Yeah."

"Great!" Keloli said. "Let's get you settled in."

–V–

"It's good to see you again," Adam said. He'd let himself in, and watched with interest as Erin stashed her meager belongings, and Deacon's, and rearranged the cabin to their liking. There wasn't much to rearrange. Two army-style bunk beds, a single wooden chair, a tiny, functional desk. Adam had a beard now, and his coal-black hair was longer. But it was neat. He didn't look like some bum.

"It was a tough decision," Erin said, glancing Deacon's way. He was sitting on one of the bunks, immersed in his second comic. Adam followed her gaze.

"Well it was a good one. For him, too." He eyed the comic book. "There are too many negative influences out there, just scrabbling for his attention."

Erin flushed. The comics were a mistake.

"I figured it would help him ease into, well, *out* of his old life," she apologized.

"No, no, that's good thinking. After he gets tired of them, we'll toss them out." Adam shook his head. "Those magazines, all they do is fight. There's no love. And look how engrossed he is in it. We're standing right here talking *about him* and he doesn't even hear us."

Deacon had been staring at the same page for several minutes without seeing it, because he couldn't stop thinking about Keloli's boobs.

When she'd leaned over to talk to him he could see right down her shirt.

She wasn't wearing a bra and he could see her boobs.

He'd seen boobs before, of course. In a magazine Dougie Cundick brought to school once (he'd paid Dougie a whole dollar for a single torn-out page of this magazine, which he'd kept hidden under his bottom dresser drawer until fear of discovery prompted him to throw it away), and another time in a movie his parents had taken him to. His father had quickly covered his eyes when the boobs appeared, but Deacon saw them for an instant and that was long enough to burn the image into his memory.

But these were the first *real* boobs he'd ever seen.

And they were glorious.

Was he in love with Keloli now? He supposed that he was. But she was *old*. Like, super old. Maybe twenty.

What was he going to do?

–VI–

"I fucking hate her," Keloli said. "*Erin*. She's got that whole 'natural' look going on, like she's some bullshit folksinger or something. She reminds me of that little slut from the Mamas and the Papas."

"That pretty, huh?" smirked Allison. Taller than Keloli by nearly a foot, she had naturally curly, chestnut hair that tumbled halfway down her back. Keloli hated Allison's hair and her long legs and especially the wise-ass smirk she currently wore.

"Pass me that fucking jay," she said. Allison handed her the joint and she took a long drag. They both lay back on Allison's bed.

"Wanna fool around?" Allison said.

"No."

"So what's the deal with the kid?"

"You know how it is. Single mom, he comes with the package." Keloli smiled. "I gave him a little show."

"How so?"

"Gave him a little peep at the twins. His jaw almost dented the ground. His dingbat mom didn't even notice." She passed the joint back to Allison and Allison finished it off.

"So are we gonna fool around or what?" Allison asked.

"I said no."

"Then get the fuck outta here. I need some me time."

"Fine," Keloli said. She paused at the door. "See you later, masturbator."

"After a while, pedophile."

–VII–

"God likes stories."

Adam paused to let that sink in. The gesture was a tad affected, but with the impenetrable blackness of night all around and the flames from the bonfire flicking bands of orange and shadow across his face, it was eerily effective.

"It explains everything. Every question you ever had. Imagine God – it doesn't even matter who or what you think that is – deciding for the first time that he wants to create life. Imagine the way any intelligent being would go about doing this if he she or it had the ability. First, you'd experiment, get the formula right. So he created microorganisms. Simple, little one-celled guys. Then he worked up to bigger and better things until he was creating complex life – purely practical in design, at first, but eventually he was creating real animals, just like the ones we have today."

Erin looked around the fire. The entire Collective was here. All seven of them. And that included herself and Deacon. Not exactly the full-blown community she'd anticipated, but it was a start. She ticked off the other girls' names in her head: Keloli, Allison, Jenny, Dena. She was terrible with names, so she made a mental note that Allison was the tall one, Jenny was the suburban housewife-next-door, and Dena was the one who looked like the prettiest – and wildest – farmer's daughter you ever saw. Actually, they were all very pretty, and Adam had them eating out of the palm of his hand, even though they'd all undoubtedly heard this spiel before.

"Then God did what any child with an exciting new toy would do," Adam continued. "He created a bunch of big, crazy-looking monsters and let them fight." He paused again, to let that sink in.

"Dinosaurs," Keloli chimed in. She clearly fancied herself his gal Friday.

"Exactly," Adam said. "Anyone who tells you that dinosaurs didn't exist because they're not in the Bible is only fooling himself."

"So God is like a big kid?" Deacon asked. Erin was surprised. She hadn't thought he was even paying attention.

"Yes!" Adam said, beyond pleased. "Exactly! He was like a big kid watching two tribes of ants fight. But his ants were gigantic monsters, and he built them himself."

"So why did all the dinosaurs die out?" Deacon asked.

"God got bored," Adam said. "He got bored, sitting around watching monsters fight all day. So he cooked up something more sophisticated. Us. His crowning achievement. Because not only are our lives little stories in themselves, but we're advanced enough to create our *own* stories in books and plays and movies.

"And God likes stories."

A couple of the girls applauded lightly.

"I still don't get how that explains everything about God though," the farmer's daughter said. Dena.

"Well, what's most people's number one question about God? *Why do bad things happen to good people*, right? Or, alternately, *Why doesn't God answer my prayers?*"

Dena nodded.

"Because he wants to see what happens. It's that simple. He wants to enjoy the *story*, and there's no story if he steps in and fixes all our problems."

"So God never answers our prayers?" Deacon asked. He sounded a little upset.

"Oh, he answers them," Adam said, tapping his forehead with his index finger. "Just not in the way we *think* we want him to."

Deacon turned to Erin. "I'm confused," he said. She put her arm around his shoulders and gave him a squeeze.

"It'll all make sense," she told him.

"It will, little man," Adam said. "But now, it's time to turn in. Erin, do you have a clear title to that car?"

The question definitely caught her off guard.

"Uh." She thought for a moment. "No. The bank has a lien on it. Ten payments left, I think?"

"We'll swap out the VIN. Allison, can you handle that in the morning? Then take it to over to the Glen and sell it to the Brothers."

"Done," Allison said.

"Wait, what?"

"We need two more space heaters for the cabins. Remember last winter?"

"So you're going to sell my car to some black guys?"

"Not those kind of brothers," Keloli said. "Actual twin brothers – Arthur and Everett. They're retarded. Literally."

"Toxic word," Adam admonished. "Yes, they are... simple. But they're not stupid, so make sure they pay you in cash."

Allison nodded.

"Keys?" Adam said, holding out his hand.

Everyone was staring at her.

"If what's ours is yours, then what's yours is also ours." Adam said. "Community."

"Or you can leave," Keloli said. "It's your choice."

Adam shot Keloli a look, but didn't say anything.

Somewhat reluctantly, Erin handed over the keys. Adam smiled.

"Welcome home," he said.

Indeed. The only way she and Deacon were getting out of here now was by walking.

It looked like they were committed.

–VIII–

It hurt.

Like a headache more intense than any you'd ever imagine possible, intermingling with a longing ache that felt like it would tear your heart right out of your chest.

If you had a heart.

Or a chest.

Yet it could see without eyes and hear without ears, so why not this almost physical longing? And why not this endless misery? It was being punished, certainly. Bound to this ugly land, in constant agony, with no real hope of ever attaining its final reward. A vague reward, the details forgotten, but one that had irrefutably been promised it.

And now this stimulation. Jealousfearhopelustcurious. Crashing in on it from seven different vectors. Awakening dimly-remembered desires and prejudices.

It sank into the earth. Not literally, of course, because it had no form. Metaphysically. Instantly, it was aware of everything within its limited sphere of influence. Despite maintaining a certain level of recognizable consciousness, it was no longer a conscious mind as we understand it. It was energy-emotion, prevented from dissipating through sheer force of will. It was as if the force generated by a machine somehow lingered after the machine had been shut off and disassembled. It was an afterimage. A stain. A smudge. It was *not* the preacher man Samuel, tragically struck down before his time. Not really.

But it didn't know this. It knew only one thing.

That it hungered.

–IX–

"There used to be a church here," Dena told her. "Like an actual Christian church."

"Really?" Erin said. They were underneath the surrounding canopy of trees, collecting detritus for firewood and loading it into a wheelbarrow that had seen better days. Deacon trailed behind, quietly poking things with a stick he'd picked up and taken a liking to. Having meticulously peeled off the soft bark in long, unbroken spirals, he'd subsequently decided that it was his walking stick.

"Yeah, in the 1910s. It was a black church, but the locals weren't having it so they burned it down. Later the hospital bought the land, then that closed down, then it was a summer camp for 'troubled youth' – whatever *that* means – and then *that* closed down."

"You sure know a lot about the area."

"Oh, I'm from here. I could walk home right now if I really wanted to. Not that I'd ever want to."

"How old *are* you?" Erin asked.

"Sixteen."

Jesus. At twenty-nine she was starting to feel like an old maid.

"Adam doesn't seem to recruit many men," Erin ventured.

"He says women are more receptive to higher ideas. Omigosh, look." Erin followed her gaze and smiled.

"Deak, look honey!"

It was a fawn. Not a hundred feet away and blithely ignoring them, it was greedily scarfing down the few remaining bits of green from a stripped bush.

"It's really late in the year to see one, Deacon," Dena said. "You're lucky."

"Where's his mom?" Deacon asked. His only experience with deer was the movie *Bambi*, and he feared the worst.

"Oh, I'm sure she's around somewhere," Erin said. "We better give him a wide berth so she doesn't get upset."

They moved on, but Deacon lagged behind, continuing to watch the baby deer. There was something... *off* about it. He froze when it suddenly looked in his direction, locking eyes with him.

Its eyes were a filmy, creamy black.

Was it sick?

They stared at each other for several seconds.

Then the deer *smiled*.

It was a malicious, knowing smile, all too human. Except for the teeth. Long and sharp, they were like a mouthful of glistening needles.

Deacon ran to catch up with his mother.

–X–

Jenny, watching from her cabin window, frowned as she watched the two women maneuver the wheelbarrow out of the woods.

"You're not giving them – us – enough to do," she said. "They've gathered enough kindling to burn down a small village. You can terrorize them, you can work them to death, you can turn this place into Camp Caligula if you want to, but you can't have them just wandering around." She turned to face a cowed Adam. "They'll get bored. They'll leave."

"They have my sermons..." he protested weakly.

"Your *sermons*. That mishmash of Gnosticism, Jesus-is-my-buddy bullshit, and cocktail party creationism? Get real."

"Keloli – Kellie – is fully dedicated. And so is Allison."

"Those two delinquents are only 'dedicated' because they think they're getting away with something." She sighed heavily. "Have you heard anything from the other two proposed subjects? The redhead and that... Chinese girl?"

"Japanese. No."

"So much for your Manson-esque charm."

"Fuck you."

"Look, I want the full dose administered to everyone tomorrow night, whether the other two show up or not. With any luck we can wrap this up and cut out by the end of the week." She turned back to the window. "I'd like to be home to take my kids trick-or-treating."

–XI–

Adam set out just before dawn, the frost-crisp grass crunching lightly beneath his feet as he made his way through the woods to the dilapidated asylum. Slipping between two two-by-fours that had been nailed just far enough apart across a doorway (on purpose, of course), he flicked on the powerful flashlight he carried and waved it around, momentarily bringing it to rest, as he always did, on the claw-foot bathtub that had fallen halfway through a water-damaged ceiling and now hung suspended above the former lobby, as if the second floor were giving birth to it.

He made his way through a swinging door to his left and, as always, obsessively counted off the doors he passed on the right side of the hallway he found himself in. One. Two. Four. Six. He stopped at six. Slowly opening it, he waved the light around.

"Boo!"

He sighed.

"I said 'Boo!'" Keloli said, stepping out of the shadows. She wore jeans and a heavy flannel shirt, although her jeans were unzipped and tugged down so that her bright red panties were showing.

"Why aren't you naked?" Adam asked, setting the flashlight end-up on the faux-marble counter so that it dimly lit the entire room. It was a patient examination room.

"Because it's fucking freezing in here," Keloli said, wrapping herself around him. "Fuck me."

"Just a minute," he said, lightly pushing her away. "Tonight we're going to have a little celebration. 'One final indulgence before casting off the bad habits that defined our former lives' or some bullshit like that. There'll be booze. You don't want to drink any of it."

"Why?"

"It's going to be spiked with a powerful hallucinogen."

"I thought you said I *didn't* want to drink it."

"You don't," he said, pulling her close and groping her. "It's a new thing, *Delta-Lysergic 2-4-9.* It bonds with specific neurons, permanently. Afterwards, it's triggered by any intense, negative emotion, amplifying said emotion a million-fold whilst simultaneously sending you on the worst trip you ever imagined."

"How bad can it be?" Keloli asked as she unzipped his trousers. She shimmied and her jeans fell down around her ankles.

"Let's put it this way. One of our chemists gave it a nickname: HellSD."

"Who did you say you worked for again?"

"I didn't."

"Tell me. It's the CIA, isn't it?"

"No."

"FBI? IRS? KGB? SPCA?"

"Stop!"

She did stop, stepping away from him.

"Tell me," she said, crossing her arms.

God damn it.

"Fine. The DBS."

"Never heard of it."

"That's *kind* of the point," he said, pulling her close again. They shared a sloppy kiss and then, kicking off her jeans, she hopped up on the examination table and stretched out on her back, moaning theatrically.

"I'm *horny* and *ripe* all the *time*, Doctor!" she cooed, writhing around. "I need an *examination!*"

He examined the shit out of her.

–XII–

"There's nothing to do here!" Deacon groaned, kicking the ground for emphasis. Erin was helping Dena lug a long, cumbersome table down the hill from the Building to the camp proper, in preparation for tonight's activities, and she really didn't have time to coddle him.

"Why don't you read your comic books again?" she tried.

"I already read them a million times."

"We can put you to work," Dena suggested.

That shut him up, but he still trailed behind them, moping. Erin signaled Dena to put the table down and made a show of wiping the non-existent sweat from her brow.

"Honey, we're really busy. We're going to have a little party tonight. That'll be fun, right?"

"That's *forever* from now."

"Well, maybe that's why you're here. To learn things like *patience*."

"You should take a walk in the woods, Deacon," Dena suggested. "Do some exploring."

Deacon remembered the baby deer.

"I don't... like the woods," he said.

"Well find something to do," Erin said, hefting her end of the table again. "Or we *will* put you to work."

Deacon made his way down the hill and paced off the perimeter of the camp, being sure to keep a safe distance from the surrounding trees. This place was so stupid. Everyone hung around all day doing nothing, then at night, instead of roasting marshmallows or singing songs or doing other fun camp stuff, they had to listen to Adam's weird, boring sermons. It was like church camp, except even church camp mixed *some* fun in with all the preaching.

In fact, the only thing he liked about this place was Keloli.

He wondered what she was doing right now.

He noticed she didn't work anywhere near as hard at the dumb, meaningless tasks Adam assigned his mom and the other girls. All she ever seemed to do was sneak off into the woods to smoke cigarettes. Emboldened by his boredom, he made his way to her cabin and, taking a deep breath, knocked lightly on the door.

She wasn't there.

Sighing inwardly – in disappointment *and* relief – he turned and nearly jumped out of his shoes when he found her standing right behind him, grinning.

"Do I have a gentleman caller?" she said.

"Uh," he said.

She laughed.

"Boys, they never change," she said good-naturedly. She waited for him to say something. When he just stood there, staring at the ground, she took the initiative. "So what brings you by my pad?"

"I dunno," he said.

"My eyes are up here." The innuendo went entirely over Deacon's head, but at least this prompted him to tear his gaze away from the ground and look in the general vicinity of her person.

"I was just kinda bored," he said with forced casualness. His voice cracked on *bored*.

"You are *adorable*," Keloli laughed, clapping her hands. He looked crestfallen so she quickly amended this. "By which I mean handsome, obviously."

He blushed. She scrutinized him for a long moment.

"Wanna take a walk?" she said.

They wandered down to the creek, were the trees were denser and, in the summer, it was dark even at midday. Now, scattered shafts of light made their way through the decimated foliage, illuminating the scores of colorful leaves lazily spiraling to the ground. Despite the bite in the air, Keloli had tied off her shirt so that her navel was exposed, and Deacon, the baby deer forgotten, stared at her belly the entire way. Now she sprawled out on the rich, dark earth next to the gurgling creek and motioned for him to sit down next to her. The ground was unpleasantly cool, and smelled earthy and moist.

"Too bad it's so chilly," Keloli sighed. "We could've gone skinny dipping."

Deacon was pretty sure his heart stopped entirely at this point, just for a second.

"Yeah," he managed.

"There's a clearing on the other side of the stream. We could sunbathe for a while." She popped the button on her jeans. "I'd have to lay out in my panties, but that's no different than laying out in a bikini bottom."

Deacon didn't respond. She was laying it on too thick, freaking him out. She decided to change tactics.

"How old are you, Deacon?" she asked.

"Twelve."

"Twelve."

"And a half," he quickly amended, instantly regretting it. That was something little kids said.

"So practically a teenager." Keloli nodded absently, as if suddenly lost in thought. "It's kinda unfair, you know? When you're ten, eleven, twelve, that doesn't count as being a teenager.

We get gypped out of three years of being a teenager." She sat up and hugged her knees. "Not that it's all it's cracked up to be," she sighed.

"How old are you?" Deacon asked, eager to fill the sudden, uncomfortable silence. He had the vague impression that he was messing this up – whatever this was – and he was pretty sure that was the last thing he wanted to do. Keloli studied him for several seconds.

"Can you keep a secret?" she asked.

Deacon nodded.

"You have to promise me something first."

"Okay."

"Promise me that, when you're older..."

"Deeeeacon!!!" His mother's voice echoed through the trees. *"Deacon, where are you?"*

"Crap," Keloli said. "You'd better get back."

"I guess." He looked heartbroken.

"Just a minute." Roughly grabbing a handful of his shirt, she pulled him close and planted one on him, right on the lips, lingering until he got over his surprise and then immediately breaking it off. "You're a good kisser," she smiled.

"Deeeeeeacon!!!!!!"

"Better go," Keloli said.

Equally reluctant and relieved, Deacon leapt to his feet and ran back to camp.

The leaves, the thing that wasn't Samuel, but could have been, decided. *I am the leaves. The leaves the leaves the leaves the leaves...*

Keloli lay back, hands behind her head, and stared at the multicolored canopy above her. She was feeling kind of horny – vamping it up and teasing boys always made her horny – but her horniness was tainted with a subtle, clinging melancholy that she couldn't quite shake. She watched the leaves flutter down with an almost zen detachment, a state of mind their self-proclaimed spiritual leader might have approved of if he wasn't, in fact, a total fraud. It's a good thing the sorry simp was so addicted to her pussy. Adam had offered up the fact that he and Jenny were feds conducting some sort of freakshow experiment the very first time he and Keloli had done it. Another potentially disastrous situation she'd successful fucked her way out of.

Maybe she should get the hell out of here now. He said they were gonna dose everybody tonight, with super acid or something. Who knows what might happen after that? Maybe they'd all go kill-crazy. Or maybe everyone would just straight-up die and then they'd shoot her because she was a witness. She didn't think Adam could actually pull the trigger on her. She'd just show him her tits. But that Jenny broad was a cold-ass bitch. Jenny played the whole "dingy suburban chick" shtick to the hilt, but she had eyes like opaque glass. Empty eyes. You should never trust anybody with empty eyes.

There was a sudden, reverberating clang

somewhere to her right, like a rock dropped onto the roof of a car from a moderate height. Gasping, she scrambled to her feet. She half-expected to find Jenny lurking, spying on her, the crazy emotionless robot-bitch having somehow read her mind from back at camp.

Nothing.

Another one, louder, behind her this time. She spun around.

There was nothing there.

Again. Again. Louder each time, all around.

A dozen, a score, more, until she was awash in a cacophony of banging, clanging, ringing, tolling...

What was happening????????

A leaf fluttered to earth right in front of her, producing a sound like a sledgehammer against a steel bulkhead as it touched down.

It was the leaves! How? How??

She covered her ears, crying out in pain as the sound of each leaf hitting the ground increased in intensity, driving her to her knees, threatening to deafen her. It felt like someone was driving ice picks into her ears. She collapsed, sobbing, fully expecting to die.

Silence.

Was she deaf? She welcomed it.

No, not deaf. She heard the dry leaves crackle beneath her as she moved. She heard a bird, somewhere, trolling for a mate.

What the fuck??? What the fuck *was* that???

Adam.

That miserable piece of shit must've dosed her already. What was going to *happen* to her? How *could* he? That *motherfucker*. That piece of fucking *shit*.

She climbed slowly to her feet, terrified to make even the slightest sound lest it be amplified to an agonizing degree. Everything seemed normal now. But for how long?

She was shaking, and she was acutely aware of the warm tears running down her face.

She closed her eyes. Deep breaths. Calming breaths.

She had to make it to the Building. She knew that's where he stashed everything. Even his super LSD, probably.

She was going to make him pay.

–XIII–

Jenny decided that if this was going to be done right, she'd better do it herself. She left Adam in charge of the other women (knowing full well he'd spend the time trying to fuck at least one of them) while she slipped out of camp, climbed the hill, and followed the winding deer trail to the old hospital.

Despite her DBS training, she wasn't aware that she had picked up a tail.

Circling around and entering through the front of the building, she hung right just past the foyer, into a hallway that led to what used to be administrative offices, now used by the "Collective" to store various odds and ends, including the non-perishable food and drink for the meeting tonight. Passing these, she came to a stop at the blank wall at the end of the hallway. Gently she pushed one of the corners, and the entire face pivoted at the center. She stepped into the hallway beyond, letting the false wall swing closed behind her. In the room hidden behind this wall was a tiny, refrigerated storage unit, about the size of a small office safe, that was not plugged into anything but nevertheless chugged contentedly, inexplicably, under its own power. She frowned with irritation as she punched in the code on the unit's illuminated keypad. Inside, stored at a constant 29 degrees, were six shatterproof glass tubes filled with a clear, thick liquid. DL2-4-9. Selecting one, she twisted off the sealed, leak-proof cap, produced a hypodermic from her shirt pocket, and, plunging the needle into the liquid, filled the hypo about halfway. More than enough. Too much, really, but it was an inert substance outside of the human body so she could safely discard the remainder anywhere. Returning through the secret wall face she let herself into the office where the items for tonight's festivities waited. Selecting three bottles of cheap/fake champagne ("Bubbly Wine!" the labels shouted) she slid the unusually thick hypodermic needle carefully through the corks and injected each bottle with exactly two cc's.

Ah, science.

A knowing smile on her face, she...

Did she just hear something?

She froze, listened intently. Any other person would have chalked it up to their imagination, but she was trained not to have that kind of imagination. If she thought someone was there, it was a good bet that someone was there. Turning slowly, she locked her eyes on the false wall and waited, counting off the seconds.

One.

Two.

Twenty.

Sixty.

Three hundred.

At two thousand she began to relax. Over thirty minutes. Amateurs weren't that patient, and a professional would have made his move by now. Double-checking that the refrigeration unit was locked, she discharged the rest of the liquid onto the filthy floor and then tossed the empty hypo into a corner. Just another piece of hospital debris.

Less than a minute later she was on the trail, on her way back to camp.

Two minutes later, Keloli slipped out of her hiding place in the office across the hall.

A secret door. How Nancy Drew.

She hadn't experienced any more hallucinations, and was becoming more confident. Maybe they'd just given her a test dose? Still unacceptable, but at least she could hold out hope that she wasn't going to end up in one of these places for real. She slid past the false wall and quickly located the refrigeration unit, incongruously new amidst all the clutter. She tugged on the handle, but it wouldn't open.

There was an alpha-numeric keypad, just like on a newer telephone. Maybe you had to punch in a combination.

F-U-C-K, Keloli tried.

Nothing.

T-I-T-S.

The door popped open.

Adam was such a fucking juvenile.

Inside, on a little stand, were five vials of clear, syrupy liquid. She picked one up and studied it. So this was Agent Adam's superdrug. Financed by the government, yet. Collecting three of the vials, she opened the other two and emptied them onto the floor. Sorry, taxpayers.

Then she backtracked to the room where all the goodies were stored. Champagne, soda, potato chips, crackers, pretzels, nuts, raisins, candy, cookies, marshmallows... In just a few years, after the Tylenol poisoning scare of 1982, many of these products would come in tamper-resistant packages. But now, in 1979, they did not. Keloli was able to contaminate a good many of them, emptying two entire vials of DL2-4-9 in the process. She slipped the third one, unopened, into her front pocket. Hallucinogens were hallucinogens. Maybe she could sell it.

Assuring herself that everything appeared kosher and unmolested, she let herself out the back way. Soon, this place would be just one more bad memory.

–XIV–

Stuffing the last of her meager belongings into her backpack, Keloli took a quick look around her cabin. God damn Adam and his hippie minimalist bullshit – there was, literally, nothing to steal. Usually when she ducked out of a situation she was able to make off with *something*, even if it was just a few bucks, or a little weed. She knew Allison had some dope stashed in her cabin, but she didn't know exactly where, and she didn't like the idea of delaying her skedaddle to look for it. Well, she'd swiped the last vial of their super acid, at least. Even if it was worthless on the street, she liked the idea that its loss might in some way inconvenience them.

Slinging the backpack over her shoulder, she peeped out her front door. No one was around.

She stepped outside and hightailed it for the treeline, walking quickly but not running, just in case anyone noticed her. Seconds later she was well within the woods, safely out of sight. Breathing a sigh of relief, she began marching, double time, and she'd put almost a mile between herself and "Asylum" before the something tugging at the back of her mind became impossible to ignore.

Deacon.

Adam and Jenny were scumbags at best. Maybe murderers. Dena and Allison were just a couple of dumb, druggie sluts, like her. But Deacon...

Ah, hell, he was just a little kid.

You're not thinking what I think you're thinking, she admonished herself.

Yeah, I am.

She stopped. If she could just force herself to start walking again, she'd probably be okay. One foot in front of the other. Repeat. That's all she had to do.

But she couldn't.

Damn.

Stashing her pack, she turned back towards camp.

Something was tapping on the window. Deacon looked up from *The Micronauts*, which he was reading for the third time in as many days. Keloli! She motioned for him to come outside and then ducked down.

He wasn't supposed to go outside.

In fact, he'd been confined to the cabin by his mom, after he refused to help prepare for tonight but nevertheless insisted on being in the way.

But there was no way he wasn't going to go talk to Keloli.

Tossing the comic aside, he went to the door and peered out. Where was she? Carefully, he slipped outside. He peeked around the corner of the cabin. There she was, motioning for him to come around back, where the cabin sat right up against the treeline and they couldn't be seen.

His hands started to shake.

"Hurry up!" she whisper-shouted.

"Hey," he said as he joined her. He was determined to play this cool. Like the Fonz.

She put her hands on his shoulders.

"Listen to me, Deacon. You – and your mom – you have to get out of here, okay? This place is no good. Adam and Jenny, they're rotten. It's like..." She thought for a second. "It's like Jim Jones, okay? Tell your mom that. Adam and Jenny are planning a Jim Jones. You have to promise me. Promise me you'll tell your mom and you'll both get out of here."

"Okay," Deacon said, baffled.

"Don't just say 'Okay,' and then go back to your comic book! Promise me!"

"Okay, I promise!" Deacon said.

"Good. You do that right now, okay? I mean *right now*."

"Are you coming with us?" Deacon asked.

"I'm booking, but not with you. Sorry." She offered him a weak smile.

Deacon looked like he wanted to say something more, but didn't. Sighing, he turned to go.

"Wait," Keloli said. "Was I your first kiss? Be honest."

"Yeah, I guess," Deacon said, making a show of shrugging his shoulders.

Grabbing his wrist, she quickly placed his hand on one of her breasts.

"Now I'm your first second base too. Tell your friends."

Before he could react she pecked him on the cheek and then disappeared into the trees.

–XV–

"Three of our marks are off the radar!" Jenny announced as she barged into Adam's cabin. He was in bed with Allison, because of course he was. "And all the 2-4-9 is gone! I've already informed Claudewell!" Adam's mouth went dry, and his penis went limp right there in Allison's hand.

"W-what?" he managed.

"He's sending in a cleanup crew."

"You can't be serious!"

In response, Jenny raised her left hand and fired the pistol she held there. The bullet made a precision hole dead center in Allison's forehead and, exiting somewhat less tidily, blew her brains and the back of her skull all over Adam, his bed, and the wall behind them.

"Jesus fucking Christ!" Adam screamed, in petulant anger rather than surprise.

"I'm deadly fucking serious," Jenny said. "But don't let me stop you." She indicated Allison's corpse with a nod. "She's still warm." Spinning on a single, bare heel, she turned and marched out of the cabin. Adam scrambled to catch up with her.

Erin believed her son, in no small part because it confirmed the prickly feeling she'd felt down her spine from the moment they got here. So she'd grabbed what she could and they ran.

Now, less than twenty minutes later, there was a massive black helicopter circling the area, like the kind that carries equipment or lots of personnel. It wasn't flying especially low, but it clearly wasn't just randomly passing over, either. Erin crouched down, motionless, and put her arm around Deacon as it circled the immediate vicinity once, twice, and then veered off in the direction of the camp. It had to be a coincidence, right? This whole setup had turned out to be so half-assed; Adam couldn't possibly have access to a *helicopter*.

"Maybe it's the police!" Deacon said.

Maybe it was. Maybe that Keloli girl had called in the cavalry.

Still, she sure as hell wasn't going to wait around to find out. She was getting her son out of here. There would be plenty of time for clarifications and an orderly, comprehensive

Q&A later.

*More of them now. They were coming en masse, like they did before. Like they **always** did.*
*This time, **he** would be triumphant.*
*This time, he would destroy them **all**.*

The helicopter hovered low over the center of camp, its rotors churning the air, blowing over the two tables the girls had set up, scattering the remnants of the previous night's bonfire. Clearing a landing area for itself. This accomplished, it set down, its body sagging visibly as gravity reclaimed its mass. Already, three heavily armed men in black bodysuits were scrambling out. They cleared the rotors and then stood at attention in front of the two agents currently in charge of the operation. The fact that one of these agents was a beautiful, barefoot woman wearing short-shorts and a tube top, and the other was a naked man wrapped in a blood-soaked bed sheet, was in no way acknowledged.

"Brink," the first man said by way of introduction. "My men are Zilch and Clever Dick."

"Clever *Rick*," the third man corrected him.

"Operation Dazzled Teakettle has been compromised and is officially an 86," Jenny told them. "I need a full cleanse. Three young women, unarmed, and a child, male, age 12. If you encounter any law enforcement, our cover story is A-5, subcat 'Rabies'." Brink nodded.

"Crack open these cabins and then spread out, standard sweep!" he ordered his two men.

Dena winced from her hiding place in one of said cabins, where she'd ducked twenty minutes ago when she first spotted a furious Jenny barreling through camp, clutching a gun.

I should've known this scene was too good to be true, she thought.

–XVI–

Amateurs in these situations almost always did two things. They followed preexisting roads and trails, even if they knew they shouldn't, and they made a beeline for the nearest population center. The latter was a straight shot north, through the woods. Brink sent Zilch and Clever Dick that way. He'd check out the trail that led to the old hospital and the road beyond himself. First, though, he'd secure the cabins.

He retrieved eight hand grenades from the helicopter. The pilot, a non-combatant who was permitted only to operate the chopper, stayed put, sucking on an unlit cigarette and leafing through a girlie magazine. Jenny followed Brink as he strolled over to the first cabin, fired a burst to shatter the front window, and then casually tossed a grenade inside. It exploded with a dull WHUMP, blowing out the other windows in a tinkle of glass.

"Clear," Brink muttered to himself. He produced a swizzle straw and stuck it in his mouth. He was a chewer. Moving on to the next cabin, he repeated the burst-grenade routine. This cabin collapsed entirely.

The door of the third cabin burst open and someone ran out, away from them, towards the treeline. Brink lifted his selective fire and peered through the scope, tracking her casually. She was just a kid, and already a looker. It was a damn shame. He put a single bullet through her left calf. Squeaking once, she went down. They approached her unhurriedly.

"Where are the others, Dena?" Jenny shouted. Brink held up a single hand to silence her. When he spoke to Dena he was calm and direct.

"We need to know where..." he looked to Jenny.

"Keloli and... uh..." She racked her brain. What was the new one's name? "Erin! Erin and Deacon."

"We need to know where Keloli, Erin, and Deacon went. Did they tell you?"

Dena shook her head.

"She's lying," Jenny said.

"She's not lying," Brink said. He lifted his weapon and put a single shot in Dena's forehead, killing her instantly. He didn't want her to suffer. She'd refrained from weeping or caterwauling, despite her leg injury, and he respected that.

"One of them is named 'Keloli'?" he asked.

"Yes," Jenny confirmed.

"That's a pretty name," Brink said, tossing a grenade through the door of the third cabin.

–XVII–

A professional always knew when someone was watching him, and someone was watching Zilch right now. He froze, carefully scrutinizing his surroundings without turning his head. Maybe one of them had doubled back. Or, more likely, had gotten lost and was just wandering around in circles. He didn't see anyone, couldn't hear anyone, but the feeling persisted, to the point where it threatened to unnerve him. That was never a good place to be, even on a cake assignment like this, and he didn't like it. Moving on, he soon reached a shallow, easily navigable stream, what the yokels he grew up with would have called a *crick*. He froze again, this time in surprise.

It was blood.

The crick was a gurgling river of blood. He could *smell* it. Kneeling down, he put his fingers in it, refusing to believe the evidence provided by his other senses.

"Jesus, Mary, and Judas," he whispered.

Whose blood was it? He automatically looked upstream, but the stream's course was almost immediately lost to a bend, obfuscated by foliage. He triggered his shoulder mic.

"Clever Dick. Zilch here. Copy."

"Clever *Rick*," came the reply. "Copy."

"You should be coming up on a little creek..."

"There now."

"You seein' what I'm seein'?"

"Seeing a creek. What are you seeing?"

Bubbles broke the surface, right in front of him. What the...?

It burst out of the water like a striking snake, but it wasn't a snake.

It was an arm. *An arm made out of blood.*

Zilch screamed as the hand at the end wrapped itself around his throat. He scrabbled at it, trying to pull it off, but his own hands passed right through the thing. It was like trying to grab hold of the water coming out of a faucet. The blood fingers were cutting off his air, but *he* somehow couldn't get a grip on *them*.

"Gahhgahh," he gasped. He was blacking out. Rolling over, he crawled away from the creek, dragging the blood arm, now disembodied, along with him. He made it almost ten feet before he lost consciousness.

"Brink. Copy."

"Brink here."

"I think Zilch is having some sort of... problem." Clever Dick did not sound sympathetic.

"What's happening?" asked Adam, in full panic mode now. He'd been up for a promotion in June. Might as well kiss *that* goodbye.

"Shut up, *Leonard*," Jenny said, using his real name.

"Am I going to have to come out there?" Brink said. He sounded like a father barking an empty threat at a pair of rambunctious children.

"Not on my account," Clever Dick responded.

"Is there anyone else out here?" Brink asked Jenny. He'd written Adam off, on sight, as someone of minimal value, possessing no useful information.

"Not that we're aware of," she said.

He frowned. Not that they were *aware* of. Not that *these* two clowns were aware of.

"We may have unidentifieds crashing this party," he informed Clever Dick. "I'm on my way. Out."

Just shy of two miles couple of miles back up the road they'd driven in on, Erin froze mid-step and pulled Deacon close.

Was that... screaming?

Just for a second, cut off almost as soon as it began.

"Erin?"

"I'm your mother," she chastised Deacon automatically. "Don't address me by my first name."

"I didn't say anything," Deacon said.

"Erin," the disembodied voice said again.

She gasped. It was Craig. Her husband. What was he doing here? What...

Moreover, *where* was he?

She looked around. The road they were on wound through a wood, sure, but the individual trees were narrow and widely-spaced, and it was broad daylight. There was nowhere a person could be hiding.

"Erin."

She caught the discrepancies this time. It *wasn't* Craig's voice. But it was close, an eerie facsimile. There was an odd, dry rustle to it, and, simultaneously, an inorganic, ethereal quality. As if it were contrived by manipulating the sound of desiccating leaves, or the wind, or the both of them in unison.

My god, what was in those woods?

–XVIII–

"You married?" asked the pilot. Brink had confined Jenny and Adam to the helicopter for the duration, and the pilot had taken an immediate interest in her.

"Yes," she said coolly.

"Happily?" he ventured.

"No, she said, looking at him pointedly. "We're on the skids and I'm looking for an out. Wanna fuck?"

The pilot frowned.

"Comedian, huh?" He turned his attention back to his magazine. "You won't be laughing when this is all over, I'll bet."

"When I want your opinion, I'll ask for it."

"No one ever wants the helicopter pilot's opinion," he said without looking up. "And yet, no one can ever get anywhere... without the helicopter pilot."

"Asshole," Jenny said, folding her arms across her chest. She didn't see him grin.

"We're fucked," Adam said for the tenth time in as many minutes. He was hugging himself, rocking back and forth. "We're royally *fucked*..."

"No," Jenny said, "*you're* fucked, because believe you me, I am going to lay this entire thing on *your* doorstep. And set it on fire."

"You're a bitch."

"Bitches are the best lays," the pilot interjected.

"Shut up, asshole!" Jenny snapped.

"Did you hear that?" Adam said.

"Yeah, she told me to shut up," the pilot said.

"No, listen."

"You're imagining things," Jenny said. "Your girlfriend probably dosed you with the Stuff. God damned amateur. Might want to check that your wallet's still there."

"No," the pilot said. "I hear it too."

Jenny listened. Now she heard it as well. A dull creaking, like stressed metal.

"What is that?" Adam squawked.

"Someone's out there, messing with the chopper," Jenny said. She glared at the pilot. "Get out there and do something!"

"I fly, that's it. Those are my orders," the pilot said. He looked nervous though.

Again, louder this time, like someone was prying a piece of the helicopter clean off.

"If something happens to this bird I'm going to make sure *you're* held responsible, not me!" Jenny hissed.

Sighing heavily, the pilot reluctantly drew his sidearm and popped open the cockpit door. Pausing, he glared back at Jenny.

"You must be the best lay ever," he said.

"*You'll* never know," she responded through a fake smile.

Shaking his head, he opened the door and cautiously stepped out.

"Stay frosty, kid," Jenny said sarcastically.

"Yeah, stay frigid," he responded.

$$-XIX-$$

Brink frowned. Zilch had been strangled to death. One-handed, it looked like. It would take an unusually massive, powerful person to do that. Not to mention quick, to close and get his hands on Zilch before Zilch was able to discharge his weapon. Frankly it didn't add up, but ignoring the facts because they didn't add up was bad field procedure. *Whys* and *hows* and *"That's impossible!"* were for the eggheads to sort out later.

So they had an unknown in play, immensely strong, and either preternaturally fast or preternaturally stealthy as well.

"Clever, copy," he said into his shoulder mic.

"Here."

"What's your location?"

"Sack-deep in a little creek north-northwest of landing site."

"I'm just upstream from you. Rendezvous with me ASAP. Zilch has been punched."

"Roger."

Clever Dick appeared moments later, wading up the center of the little stream. He joined Brink next to the body.

"What do you think?" Brink asked him.

"An EGW containment's always full of surprises."

"No, this is something else..." Brink looked slowly around the wood, then closed his eyes and listened. To the gently laughing brook. To the leaves, their rustling like distant, polite applause. It was as if the place itself were slyly mocking them, cheering on whatever was happening. "There's something here all right," he said, opening his eyes. "I think maybe we stirred something up."

"The Folk?" Clever Dick ventured.

"I don't think so. Maybe something para."

"I ever tell you about the time my mom saw the ghost of my grandma?"

"This isn't the ghost of your grandma."

Pulling out is what the zit-faced punk fucking your little sister does when he's all out of condoms, his drill instructor used to say. *Marines do not pull out.*

Sorry Sarge, but sometimes discretion really is the better part of valor.

"Fall back to the chopper."

Keloli froze. There was something flitting through the spaces between the trees, through the spaces *between* the spaces. A blot, there but not there, like a translucent stain on a piece of glass that had been laid over the scene in front of her. She closed her eyes and shook her head, trying to dismiss it. But when she opened them it was still there, to her right now, circling, circling... Icy, invasive tendrils of thought penetrated her mind and she suddenly knew that this... *thing* wanted to have sex with her. No, it wanted to *hurt* her. Physical copulation was just the means to that end. Now it was in front of her again, now to her left. Never behind. It was herding her.

Damn it. She shut her eyes against it again.

It wasn't there.

It was all in her head.

She took a tentative step forward. Another.

Her mind grew heavy with guilt, unfocused but overpowering. Everything she had ever done wrong came flooding back and she despaired.

I'm going to go to Hell, she thought. This conclusion was so indisputable, the implications so all-encompassing, that she began to weep.

Then the feeling was gone. Just like that.

She opened her eyes.

The blot was gone too. But...

Copulation.

The word hung there, like a song you can't get out of your head.

Keloli had fucked her share of guys. She'd screwed guys and banged guys and hooked up with guys.

But she didn't *copulate* with guys.

Something had planted that word in her brain. Something from outside.

She wasn't hallucinating. There was something here.

Something evil.

She almost laughed at the absurd melodrama inherent in that statement.

Almost.

–XX–

"Errrrriiiinnnn....."

The voice was like an old piece of wood bent just shy of its breaking point. The weary groan of dead organic material. She covered her ears.

"Mom?" Deacon said. He didn't hear anything.

Cracks. Pops. Shriveled leaves crushed underfoot. Sticks and dried thorn bushes snapping. Dead things further destroyed because being dead simply wasn't enough.

Not for It.

Erin bolted in blind, unreasoning terror. Nothing else mattered, not even her boy, who stared, agape, as she left him behind. She just ran, away from the vague horror before her, back towards the perceived safety of the campsite.

Exactly where it wanted her to go.

The sound had stopped. He did a circuit around the entire whirlybird. Nothing. Glancing through the 'bird's window, he saw the faces of his two charges pressed against it, watching him. He lowered his weapon and shrugged his shoulders theatrically for their benefit.

Something had hold of his foot. He looked down. Roots. Somehow he'd gotten his right foot entangled in them, and even as he watched they seemed to move of their own accord, tightening their grip. He tugged the foot free and then watched, amazed, as the thick roots rapidly disappeared into the ground. Five of them, like the fingers of a hand.

Only then did he see it. Similar clumps had grown up and around all three wheels of the chopper, gripping it as if they were working in unison to hold it down. They weren't strong enough to do that, of course, but that wasn't what worried him. What freaked him out was: How could they grow so fast? Even as he watched, they crept up over the wheels and wrapped themselves higher and tighter around the gear. His gut reaction was to fire his weapon into them, but that didn't make a lick of sense.

The lament of stressed metal again, louder this time, coming from everywhere and nowhere.

He looked back to the window but the two faces weren't there anymore. He heard them clambering out the other side of the chopper.

"You stay right here!" he called out, his eyes

still on the climbing, snaking vegetation.

The cockpit window suddenly spider-webbed with a dull *pop*.

The two idiots scampered around the aircraft to join him.

The entire chopper was shimmying now, rocking back and forth, faster and faster. The primary rotors turned one full rotation, slowly, of their own accord.

Then, instantly, it stopped. The shaking, the sound, all of it. The sudden, unexpected silence was punctuated dramatically by a distant, calling bird.

"What. The. Fuck?" said Adam.

"It's the Stuff," Jenny said. "The fucking 2-4-9."

"Bullshit!" Adam shouted. "We all saw that! People don't share the same hallucination!"

"*Folie à trois*," Jenny said.

"This is no time to be thinking about fucking two dudes!" Adam groaned.

She turned and considered him, hoping against hope that he was using lowbrow humor to cope with an untenable situation. But no, from all appearances he really was that stupid.

"You think we're hallucinating?" the pilot asked.

"That's on a need-to-know basis," she said.

He briefly considered shooting her.

⌘⌘⌘

There was a crow watching them, perched nonchalantly on a wire, its head swiveling to follow them as they marched back to the camp. Except, Brink realized, there was no wire. It was just sitting there, claws wrapped around nothing, hovering in midair. He froze and held up a hand so that Clever Dick came to a halt too. The crow was filthy, appeared to be molting, and its eyes writhed with movement. He lifted a pair of field 'nocs to get a better look. Maggots. Its eyes were gouged out and the sockets were filled with black, squirming maggots. This didn't seem to bother it though, and it stared back at him arrogantly, as if its ability to see was in no way compromised by its sorry condition.

"Clever, shoot that fucking bird," Brink ordered. "I want to see what happens."

Clever Dick raised his weapon but even as he did the crow took flight, circled them once, and then vanished. Literally, like picture projector that had suddenly been shut off.

"Fuck me," Clever said.

"Something's definitely riled up here," Brink said. "Either we're trespassing, as it sees things, or because of all the killing. We'll have to stop shooting people."

Clever Dick frowned slightly at this.

"We'll fall back to the chopper," Brink went on. "Report in and go from there."

Motion in his peripheral vision. He turned and saw a young girl, attractive (though more sexy than pretty), picking her way through the brush, headed in their general direction. She saw them a moment later and raised her hands in surrender. A random hiker wouldn't have done that. She was one of theirs.

"Collect her and then follow me," Brink said.

–XXI–

Brink and Clever Dick emerged from the northwest treeline with Keloli in tow. Jenny briefly wondered why they hadn't shot the little snot, but then reasoned that maybe she knew which way the other two had gone and they planned to interrogate her. With any luck, torture would be necessary.

"You won't believe..." Adam began but Brink held up a single hand to silence him. Jenny, however, was not so easily intimidated.

"We've been dosed," she said. "Somehow we've all ingested the..." She glanced at the pilot. How much was he savvy to? For that matter, how much were the cleaners savvy to? Maybe she shouldn't have said anything.

"Negatory," Brink said, saving her from any

further explanation. "Whatever you've been doing out here, what we're experiencing now is, at best, an indirect result." He studied the landing gear of their chopper, now fully encased in a thick, clinging weave of roots. "Can this bird pull free?" he asked the pilot.

"Absolutely."

"Okay. Fire it up. Clever, cuff the girl. Everybody get on board."

A scream cut across the clearing, its source immediately obfuscated by its own multi-directional echo. Erin.

"We have to go help them!" Keloli pleaded.

Brink actually seemed to consider this, then dismissed the idea.

"No. We're..." he grimaced, as if the words pained him "...pulling out."

Erin tore through the underbrush, heedless of the thorn bushes scratching her bare arms and the branches whipping her in the face. *"Errrriiiinnnn..."* the dry, dead voice, almost but not her husband's, called after her. *"Errriiinnn... where's Deacon... where's our SON...?"*

"You can have him! You can have him! Just don't take *me!*" she sobbed. Desiccated shrubs entangled her like dry barbed wire, but they were fragile in death and she easily tore them away, although their thorns left her hands slick with blood.

"Erin." Ahead of her now.

"Erin." Behind her again.

"Erin." In the leaves, on the wind, all around, everywhere.

There was no place to run. Hopelessness descended upon her and she fell to her knees.

"While you're down there..." Craig always used to say whenever she knelt or bent over for any reason whatsoever. How she hated his witless, accompanying smirk. How she hated *him*, and everything he brought into her previously carefree life.

Even Deacon.

The admission broke her, and she wept.

Now something was coming. Something assembled of hate and sorrow. Something that had waited patiently for this very moment to pounce. It enveloped her, cold, clinging, damp, accompanied by the smell of rotting wood. The impression of fingers, wet, semi-solid, stroking her cheek. Their ghostly non-substance penetrated her skull and plucked the strings of her mind like a guitarist plunks the strings of his instrument. Then, one by one, she felt each of her mental strings break.

She stared blankly ahead, seeing nothing, a single rivulet of drool dribbling down her slack jaw.

Mine... sighed the wind.

But first...

While you're down there...

–XXII–

"It won't turn over," said the pilot.

"Alright," said Brink, "radio it in."

The pilot tried the radio, then gave Brink a look that said it all.

"Am I under arrest?" Keloli asked. "Where are Dena and Allison?" Brink ignored her.

"Okay," he said, "we walk out. Clever, you take point. I'll need someone to take charge of the girl..."

"I'll do it," said Jenny.

"Look," interrupted the pilot, pointing towards the treeline. There was a woman standing there, naked. Erin.

"That's one of ours," said Jenny.

"Clever, fetch," said Brink. "No violence."

"Roger," Clever said, bounding out of the

chopper and jogging towards Erin.

"Just shoot her!" Jenny said, exasperated.

"No!" shouted Keloli. *"Erin, run!"*

"Quiet her down," Brink said.

Jenny slugged Keloli in the stomach, hard enough to double her over. Unable to maintain her balance with her hands cuffed behind her back, she fell to the ground.

"Not like that!" Brink snapped. "No violence!"

"What, are we Gandhi now?"

The naked woman's eyes followed Clever Dick as he trotted towards her, the faintest of smiles touching her lips, but otherwise she stood as motionless as a statue. She was ridiculously pretty, he realized, one of the prettiest women he had ever seen. Yet there was something off about her. Dismissing the thought, he slung his weapon over his shoulder and produced a set of handcuffs. "Hands behind your back, please," he said.

"Do you want me?" the girl whispered, somewhere between a coo and a wistful sigh.

"I want you to put your hands behind your back," he said.

"Yes," he said.

Wait, what?

"I need you to put your hands behind your back," he repeated. He was sure of it.

"I want you so much," is what he actually said.

She stepped into him and threw her arms around his neck. He closed his eyes and drew her close. Her lips pressed against his. He was so aroused it was actually painful.

"Clever! That's an order!" someone was shouting. Someone from a long time ago, a voice from his distant past that didn't matter anymore.

Her tongue was in his mouth now, but it was a cold, wet slug and he knew he'd been deceived but it was too late and he no longer cared. She fumbled at his belt, his pants, and then they were around his knees and he was inside her and he wept for the joy of it, even as her teeth sank into his tongue and her fingers found his eyes and plunged into them up to the second knuckle. A shot rang out, the bullet splinter-popping a gash in a tree just to the left of Erin's head. A wild shot fired by the helicopter pilot. Erin released Clever Dick and he sank to the earth, spewing fluids from nearly every orifice. His body thrashed once, twice, and then was still. Through it all, he never stopped smiling.

Screw it, Brink decided, raising his weapon. The "woman" was striding purposefully towards them, pausing only so spit something pink and organic out of her mouth. Clever Dick's severed tongue. *"It's not real! It's not real!"* Jenny shrieked. Brink caught a whiff of vomitus and assumed, correctly, that Adam was the one puking, but he couldn't hear the retching because now he was pumping round after round into the approaching thing. Whatever was driving didn't appear unduly concerned by this, but by the time it had closed half the distance he'd put so many holes in the body it had commandeered that said body was functionally useless. It crumpled to the ground and was still.

"Oh my god oh my god oh my god..." their prisoner was chanting.

"Uncuff her," Brink told the pilot.

"What's happening?" Adam sobbed.

"Don't you dare uncuff her," Jenny said, pointing her handgun at Brink. "We're not doing this, this 'the enemy of my enemy is my friend' bullshit. If you can't bring yourself to eliminate these civilians I'll do it for you."

Brink hesitated, something he was hardly known for. She was right, of course, but these were extenuating circumstances. Weren't they? He wished his thoughts weren't so muddled...

"Something's coming!" Adam wailed.

Shapes, in the trees. Figures approaching them, scores of them. Some walking, some shambling, some gliding inches about the earth, their feet dangling unused beneath them. There was an African-American, hulking, furious, his eyes pale and gleaming. A woman with the head of a buck deer, its intricate latticework of antlers draped with cobwebs and hanging moss. Some of them, they recognized. Keloli's hated stepfather was there. The man who had raped Jenny at a high school party and was now a decorated war hero. At least a dozen people Brink had killed over the course of his career. Others they might have known, like Dena's parents, and Erin's estranged husband Craig, and a popular musician wearing studded boots and cartoonish black and white makeup. Brink and Jenny both opened fire on the advancing throng, to no avail. Adam collapsed in a heap on the ground, wailing. The pilot bolted in the wrong direction and was immediately cut down by friendly fire.

Keloli, her hands still cuffed behind her back, managed her way back into the helicopter and curled up in a ball, waiting to die.

–XXIII–

Silence. For several minutes now. Cautiously, Keloli peeped outside. Nothing. No phantasms, no monsters, no ghosts from her (or anyone else's) past. Just four bodies – Adam, Jenny, the pilot, and that other guy. The pilot had been perforated to shit but the other three didn't have a visible mark on them. Keloli huddled there, too frightened to move, for nearly an hour, but when nothing happened in that time she was emboldened to clamber out of the helicopter and flee. First, though, she sat down and slipped her ass and legs through her cuffed hands so that they were bound in front of her now. It paid to be limber. She started walking.

Fifteen minutes later she found Deacon, huddled in the lengthening shadow of the old asylum, tears still glistening on his face. He hugged her tight for a long time and they continued on together. When they heard the sound of a second helicopter they hid in the woods and waited as it passed over, followed immediately by two black panel vans with no markings that tore past them on the narrow dirt road, headed towards the camp. As dusk fell they came upon an isolated house, the front yard dense with disused tools and dilapidated machinery, and when the addled coot who lived there satisfied himself that they weren't trying to "bogart his stash" he agreed to cut Keloli's handcuffs off in exchange for a handjob, negotiated down from a blowjob. She'd done more for less, and she managed to steal his wallet in the process, so she chalked the interaction up as a win. By morning they'd reached civilization, of a sorts. A town, at best, aspiring to be one-horse, sporting a single stoplight and one lonely phone booth.

"We gotta call somebody," she told Deacon.

"Not my dad."

"Okay." She sighed. "We can't call my parents either."

Deacon sniffled.

"Don't worry, Deak." She took his hand and gave it a gentle squeeze. "We'll think of something."

Eventually, they did.

⌘ ⌘ ⌘

The four researchers who were riding in the black panel vans took sample after sample from the bodies of Jenny, Adam, Brink, and the helicopter pilot before instructing the enlisted men who had accompanied them to incinerate the remains with flamethrowers. The compromised helicopter was given the business as well, and then the entire area was set ablaze, igniting a forest fire that would burn for several days and ultimately claim the lives of three.

The researchers departed in the second chopper while the enlisted men finished the job.

"Pretty efficient," said Collins. He was the new guy, a last-minute replacement for Milstrom, who'd gotten himself killed in a hit-and-run while walking to the corner market for a pack of cigarettes.

"Efficient *and* promising," said Drake. "Aside from the one who got himself shot, they all appear to have died from heart failure. Exactly as we anticipated."

"How long was the 2-4-9 in their systems before it kicked in?" Collins asked. He still wasn't entirely up to speed on the project.

"Oh, months. From their initial assignment, even before they set up their little 'cult' and started collecting the control group. The supposed test subjects were actually the control, and the so-called administrators were actually the test subjects. See?"

Collins nodded.

"So much easier to induce stress in uptight go-getters like..." he referred to his notes "...this 'Brink' chap and this 'Jennifer Marsailes'. Type A's are notoriously fragile when their expectations go off the rails."

"Pretty ingenious," said Collins.

"*Ingenious* is our job description."

NOW

"There was a really bad fire here back in 1979," Amos said.

"Oh yeah?" said Janke, clearly disinterested. That was twenty years before he was born, and he had little interest in anything that happened that long before he was born.

"Yup," Amos went on, half-assedly pounding the last sign into the ground. "A firefighter died, some other people. I was just a little kid but I remember because they evacuated us in case the wind changed and it came towards town. We stayed in a hotel and I thought it was this big adventure."

"Uh huh." Janke took a long look around. It sure didn't look like there'd ever been a fire here. But maybe that's why the trees were so much smaller than the ones over the hill – they were younger. Made sense.

"They say it's haunted," Amos added.

"Bullshit."

"No bullshit. People've seen things, heard things. Even the high school kids won't come out here on dares or to scare their dates out of their pants. That's when you know it's for real."

"You wouldn't know for real if it bit you on your fat ass," Janke said, climbing into the passenger seat of the city truck. Amos joined him.

"Just for that, you're buying." Amos started the engine and they pulled out, much to Janke's relief. No way he'd admit it to that fat fuck in a thousand years, but this place really did give him the creeps.

The last sign they'd planted canted slightly, but didn't fall down. "CONDOS FROM $160,000 – PRE-SALES BEGIN FEB. 1st!" it read.

Here Comes Love Bloom and Six!

♥

www.ingramcontent.com/pod-product-compliance
Lightning Source LLC
Chambersburg PA
CBHW020326180726

47991CB00019B/879